**Put Beginning Readers on the Right Track with
ALL ABOARD READING™**

The All Aboard Reading series is especially for beginning readers. Written by noted authors and illustrated in full color, these are books that children really and truly *want* to read—books to excite their imagination, tickle their funny bone, expand their interests, and support their feelings. With three different reading levels, All Aboard Reading lets you choose which books are most appropriate for your children and their growing abilities.

Level 1—for Preschool through First Grade Children
Level 1 books have very few lines per page, very large type, easy words, lots of repetition, and pictures with visual "cues" to help children figure out the words on the page.

Level 2—for First Grade to Third Grade Children
Level 2 books are printed in slightly smaller type than Level 1 books. The stories are more complex, but there is still lots of repetition in the text and many pictures. The sentences are quite simple and are broken up into short lines to make reading easier.

Level 3—for Second Grade through Third Grade Children
Level 3 books have considerably longer texts, use harder words and more complicated sentences.

All Aboard for happy reading!

For Chloe and Sam — A.G.

In memory of my dad,
who taught me to love baseball — B.F.

Special thanks to Bill Deane, Senior Research Associate,
National Baseball Hall of Fame and National Baseball Library

Photo credits: pp. 4-5, 8, 26, National Baseball Library, Cooperstown, NY; pp. 6, 9, 12, 17, 21, 31, 35, 38, UPI/Bettmann; pp. 41, 44 (left), Reuters/Bettmann; pp. 34, 42, John Iacono/*Sports Illustrated*; p. 44 (right), © 1992 TV Sports Mailbag Inc./Photo File, Elmsford, NY 10523.

Library of Congress Cataloging-in-Publication Data

Gutelle, Andrew.
  All-time great World Series / by Andrew Gutelle ; illustrated by
Bart Forbes.
     p.   cm. — (All aboard reading)
  1. World Series (Baseball)—History—Juvenile literature. [1. World Series (Baseball)
  2. Baseball.] I. Forbes, Bart, ill. II. Title. III. Series.
  GV878.4.G88 1994
  796.357′646—dc20   93-35668
                                                                          CIP
ISBN 0-448-40472-9 (GB)   A B C D E F G H I J   AC
ISBN 0-448-40471-0 (pbk.) A B C D E F G H I J

ALL
ABOARD
READING™
Level 3
Grades 2-3

ALL-TIME GREAT
WORLD
SERIES

By Andrew Gutelle
Illustrated by Bart Forbes

With photographs

Grosset & Dunlap • New York

October 1, 1903

It is a beautiful fall afternoon in Boston—perfect baseball weather. The Boston Pilgrims are set to battle the Pittsburgh Pirates. But this is no ordinary ball game. Sports history is about to be made. This is the first game of the first American League–National League World Series!

The stands are packed. Fans spill onto the field. They even stand behind the outfielders. The first pitch has not even been thrown. But the World Series is already a hit.

Fans pack the field for the 1903 World Series.

Since that very first game, the World Series has become baseball's biggest show. A key hit or a costly error can make—or break—a player forever. That's why fans love to watch "The Fall Classic."

Here are the stories of four of the most exciting World Series. Each one is filled with great players, great plays, and great big surprises. Each one is a classic!

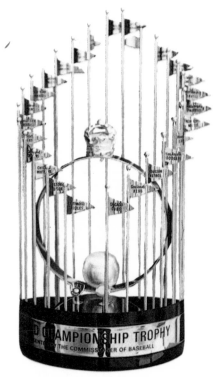

The World Series Trophy

1

The Big Train Rumbles Home

"First in war, first in peace and last in the American League!" For years, that's what people have been saying about Washington, D.C. and its baseball club. The Senators have been baseball's worst team. A sports joke.

But not in 1924. This year Washington wins ninety-two games and finishes first. At last, the Senators will play in the World Series!

The star of the team is pitcher Walter Johnson. Walter was a shy farm boy when he joined the Senators in 1907. Since then his blazing fastball has become the toughest pitch to hit in baseball. Hit it? Sometimes batters can't even see it!

Johnson is a favorite
of fans everywhere.
They call him
"The Big Train"
because of the
excitement fans feel
when Johnson roars
into town.

In 1924, Johnson is
thirty-six years old.
He is almost at the end
of his career. At times,
his fastball loses its sizzle.
Still, he's had a great
season so far. Fans
everywhere are rooting
for Walter. They want
to see "The Big Train"
win the World Series.

Walter Johnson

Johnson's job will not be easy. The Senators are facing the powerful New York Giants. The Giants are playing in their fourth straight World Series. The team is loaded with great players, including third baseman Freddie Lindstrom. He is only eighteen years old, the youngest person ever to play in a World Series.

Young Freddie Lindstrom

Fans pack Griffith Stadium in
Washington to watch Johnson open the
Series. Babe Ruth and Ty Cobb are there.
So is President Calvin Coolidge. People
without tickets crowd into nearby
apartment buildings. They will watch
today's action from the rooftops.

President Coolidge throws out the first
ball. Then Johnson takes the mound.

Walter is sharp today. But he faces an
awesome lineup. Two home run blasts give
the Giants an early lead. The Senators fight
back. In the ninth inning, they tie the
score.

"The Big Train" on the mound.

Johnson is tiring. But the Senators stick with their ace into extra innings. Johnson strikes out two Giants in the tenth. He whiffs another batter in the eleventh. Then in the twelfth, the Giants load the bases.

Johnson gets one out. He gets another. But the Giants rack up two runs to take the lead. The Senators come back with a run of their own. But it is not enough. It is a tough loss for Walter.

Johnson's next turn comes in game five. The Series is tied at two wins each. But again, Walter is not at his best. The Giants knock out thirteen hits. They beat Johnson and the Senators 6–2.

The Giants need just one more victory to clinch the Series. But the Senators refuse to give up. Back home in Washington, they win game six. The Series is tied again. The seventh and final game will decide it all.

Sadly, the Senators must try to win without Johnson. One day of rest is not enough time to get the zip back in Walter's fastball. He quietly takes his seat at the end of the bench.

The Senators grab an early lead. But in the sixth inning, the Giants come back. They pick up three runs and seem to take control of the game.

Now it's the eighth inning. The Senators load the bases. The next batter hits a grounder to Giants third baseman Freddie Lindstrom. It's a big moment for the eighteen-year-old. But just as it reaches him, the ball takes a strange bounce. It hops right over his head! The Senators score two runs to tie the game.

The fans are still cheering when the ninth inning begins. The Senators know they cannot let the Giants score. Washington Manager Bucky Harris calls for a new pitcher. Who does he want? Walter Johnson!

The manager hands him the ball. "You're the best we've got, Walter," he says. "We've got to win or lose with you."

Johnson goes to work. With one out he gives up a triple. But he settles down and gets two more outs.

Still tied, the game goes into extra innings. Can Walter keep it up? Giant batters get on base inning after inning. But Johnson pitches his way out of every jam.

The Senators bat in the last of the twelfth. The second batter hits a double. Now it's Johnson's turn to face the pitcher. He hits a grounder to the shortstop, who bobbles the ball. Johnson is safe on first!

The fans are on their feet. A single will win the game. For the Senators, it's now or never. The next batter hits a grounder to third. Young Freddie Lindstrom is ready to catch it. But at the last instant the ball strikes a pebble. The ball takes a wild hop over Freddie's head—<u>again</u>! The runner scores. The Senators win the Series!

An older Freddie Lindstrom relives the famous bounce.

After the game, Walter Johnson is tired but happy. "If I never pitch another ball game, I will have this one to remember and I'll never forget it," he says.

In fact, Johnson hangs on. He pitches for three more seasons before retiring in 1927. And in 1936, "The Big Train" becomes one of the first players to roar into the brand-new Baseball Hall of Fame.

2

Reggie! Reggie! Reggie!

During the 1940s and 1950s, the New
York Yankees and Brooklyn Dodgers are
baseball's best-known hometown rivals.
New York City fans ride the subway from
Yankee Stadium in the Bronx to Ebbets
Field in Brooklyn. They watch their teams
square off in seven World Series. These
"Subway Series" include many great
games. The Yankees and Dodgers seem to
bring out the best in each other.

Then in 1957, the Dodgers move west.
The Brooklyn "Bums" become the Los
Angeles Dodgers. But the old rivalry never
dies! Twenty years later, the New York
Yankees and the Los Angeles Dodgers meet
again. In 1977, it's East against West to see
who is baseball's best.

The Yankees can hardly wait. They have a mighty new weapon: Reggie Jackson! While playing for the Oakland A's, the slugging outfielder led his team to three World Series championships. No one hits a ball farther than Jackson. And Reggie is fearless. The tougher the spot, the better he plays.

Jackson is also a cocky player. Some of his teammates are jealous of him. And Yankee manager Billy Martin doesn't like him. But when Reggie is finally put in the cleanup spot, everyone agrees on one thing. He gets the job done.

When the Series starts, the Yankees and Dodgers split the first two games in New York. Then they fly west for three games in Dodger Stadium. The National League champs hope to take charge at home. But the Yankees grab games three and four. The Dodgers win game five to keep the Series alive. But just barely.

The last two games will be in Yankee Stadium. New York needs just one win to clinch the title. "No way we lose twice at home," boasts Jackson.

The sixth game seesaws from inning to inning. The Dodgers jump in front in the first. Then the Yankees tie it up in the second. The Dodgers go back ahead in the third.

Now it's the fourth inning. Yankee catcher Thurman Munson leads off with a single. Reggie Jackson steps up to the plate. The pitcher throws a fastball. But Reggie is ready. He whips his bat across home plate. As he connects, the ball jumps off the bat. An instant later, it lands in the right field stands. Jackson's first swing is a home run. The Yanks lead!

Reggie Jackson shows off his home run swing.

One inning later, Jackson steps up to the plate again. The pitcher tries to bust a fastball close to Jackson's hands. Reggie swings. C-r-r-a-a-c-k! <u>Another</u> line drive lands in the right field stands. Two swings. Two home runs! New York fans are on their feet.

Jackson leads off in the eighth inning. This will be his final at bat. The scoreboard flashes: REG-GIE REG-GIE.

Fifty-six thousand fans pick up the chant.

The Dodgers send a new pitcher to the mound. His name is Charlie Hough. He throws knuckleballs that dip and dart as they float over home plate. This tricky pitch is tough to throw. It is even tougher to hit.

Reggie takes a practice swing. Then he steps into the batter's box. The scoreboard flashes another message: ONE MORE TIME!

Hough winds up. He sends his first knuckleball fluttering to the plate. Jackson swings. He drops his bat. He watches the ball sail toward center field. Back, back, it goes. Over the fence. Three swings. Three home runs!

As Jackson trots around first base, he holds up three fingers to the fans. Smiling, he circles the other bases. Then he steps on home and heads for the dugout. Billy Martin hugs him. His teammates surround him. Today no one is jealous. Today everybody loves Reggie!

The game goes on, but the crowd will not stop cheering. Jackson steps out of the dugout. He takes off his batting helmet and waves to the fans one more time.

One inning later, the game ends. The
Yankees are champions. And Reggie
Jackson has earned the nickname "Mr.
October." He is only the second player to
hit three home runs in a World Series
game. The other is the most famous
Yankee of all—Babe Ruth. Even Jackson is
stunned by what he has done. "I was just
lucky," says Reggie, modestly. "Babe Ruth
was great."

The great
Babe Ruth

3

Mookie's Bouncer Bops Sox

Luck plays a part in every sport. And during the 1986 World Series, fans witnessed one of the luckiest moments in baseball history. Was it good luck or bad luck? Well, that depends if you were rooting for the Boston Red Sox or the New York Mets.

The Mets and the Sox are baseball's best teams in 1986. And each team is eager for their shot in the World Series.

The Mets always seem to shine in the World Series. In 1969, the "Amazin' Mets" shocked the baseball world with their first Series win. Four years later, they nearly whipped the mighty Oakland A's. In 1986, New York fans are sure the Mets are ready to win it all.

For the Sox, on the other hand, the Series has meant mostly bad luck. In 1903, as the Boston Pilgrims, they won. But in the last 68 years, they have lost three heartbreaking Series. Boston fans wonder: Is their team jinxed? Or will 1986 finally end their losing streak?

When the World Series opens in New York, the Red Sox are red-hot. They win the first two games. The Mets just can't seem to keep up.

The scene moves to Boston for game three. And the Mets rally. Led by the home run hitting of Len Dykstra and Gary Carter, they win two out of three games in Boston. The teams return to New York for the final showdown.

Still, Boston is ready to win it all. They lead three games to two. One win away from their first championship in sixty-eight years. It looks like their luck has finally changed.

Roger Clemens will pitch for the Sox in game six. Boston does not want to play a seventh game. They want to win this one with their ace on the mound.

Pitcher Roger Clemens is dazzling. "The Rocket" strikes out six Mets in the first three innings. In fact, everything is going Boston's way.

But the Mets fight back and tie the score. After nine innings, the game is still tied.

Dave Henderson leads off the tenth inning for the Sox. He swings at the second pitch. Smack! It sails over the left field wall for a home run. The tie is broken! Boston is back on top.

The Red Sox add another run to lead 5-3. They're <u>sooooo</u> close. They can almost taste victory.

The Mets try to rally in the bottom of the tenth. But after two fly balls, they are only one out away from losing. The Red Sox are one out away from winning it all. It looks like <u>both</u> teams' luck has changed.

Sox fans everywhere are already beginning to celebrate. But there is an old baseball saying: It ain't over till it's over.

First Gary Carter smacks a single to left. Then Mets pinch hitter Kevin Mitchell raps a single to center. The tying runs are on base!

Ray Knight is next. He hits a soft line drive for a single. Carter scores. Mitchell races to third. The score is 5–4. It's a one-run game!

Boston changes pitchers in the middle of the inning. Reliever Bob Stanley's best pitch is a sinkerball. If he can use this low pitch to get a ground ball out, the inning will be over. The Series will be theirs!

The Mets' next batter is Mookie Wilson. He steps up to the plate. Stanley pitches. Mookie swings. And misses. "No big deal," Mookie tells himself. "Just cool down and relax."

Mookie works the count to two balls and two strikes. When the next pitch comes, he hits it foul. Then he hits <u>another</u> foul. Mets fans are getting more nervous with each pitch.

Bob Stanley fires a pitch to Mookie Wilson.

Bob Stanley's inside pitch heads for Mookie Wilson's foot.

Mookie is reaching over the plate on every swing. So Stanley decides to slip a sinker low and inside. The ball nearly hits Mookie's foot. But he jumps away. The ball bounces and skips off the catcher's glove. Then it rolls back toward the stands.

"Let's go, Mitch!" shouts Mookie. And Kevin Mitchell dashes home. The Mets tie the game. Again!

Mookie is <u>still</u> at bat. He hits <u>another</u> foul. And <u>another</u>! Finally, on the tenth pitch, Mookie swings and hits a soft ground ball to first base.

The ball takes two high hops. Then it bounces low over the base. First baseman Bill Buckner bends down for an easy catch and the third out. Then the impossible happens. The ball rolls <u>under his glove</u>!

As Ray Knight rounds third, he sees the ball go between Buckner's legs. There is no stopping him as he gallops across home plate. The Mets win! The Series is tied! The Red Sox are stunned!

Two days later, Bruce Hurst takes the mound for Boston. He has already won two World Series games. This is their last chance. Can Hurst rescue the Red Sox?

The answer is <u>no</u>. Boston's luck has run out. The Mets roar back one final time. In three innings, they score eight runs. In the eighth inning, Darryl Strawberry cracks a long home run. Then the Mets add one last run. The scoring is finished. And so are the Red Sox.

Once again, the World Series has brought out the best in the Mets. And the Red Sox? Their fans still say they're the most unlucky team in baseball!

The Mets celebrate their Series-winning run.

4

The Greatest Ever?

Imagine the most exciting World Series of all time. Two unlikely teams. Seven tight games. Who will win? The answer swings from game to game, and inning to inning. Finally, one team squeaks by. Barely. Welcome to the 1991 World Series.

In eighty-eight years, no American or National League team has ever gone from last place one year to first place the next. But in 1991 it happened. Twice!

The Atlanta Braves are the National League champs. The Braves are in their first World Series since they played in Milwaukee in 1958.

1990

65 wins
97 losses

1991

94 wins
68 losses

The Minnesota Twins won the World Series in 1987. But since then, they have fallen way back. By 1990, they are in the cellar. The next winter, the team adds several key players. Amazingly, the club bounces back. In 1991, they win the American League pennant.

1990

74 wins
88 losses

1991

95 wins
67 losses

The 1991 World Series opens at the Metrodome in Minnesota. The Twins have never lost a World Series game in this ballpark. In the first two games, the streak continues. It's 2–zip for the Twins.

The scene shifts to Atlanta. The teams battle back and forth in game three. The Twins go out in front. Then the Braves take the lead. In the eighth inning, the Twins tie up the game. And it stays tied until the twelfth inning, when Atlanta second baseman Mark Lemke singles and sends Dave Justice home. The game goes to the Braves!

Mark Lemke's teammates congratulate him.

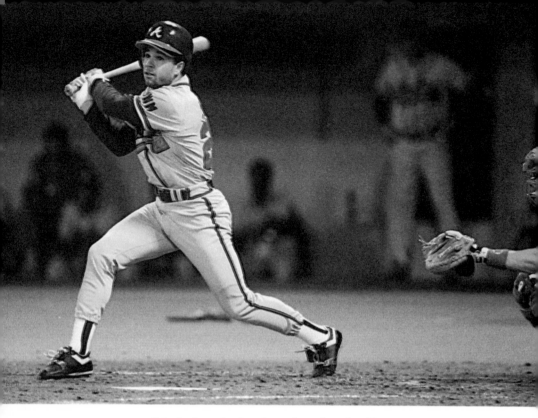
Mark Lemke back to bat for the Braves.

Lemke keeps the Braves rolling. In game four, he triples in the ninth and scores the winning run. In game five, he drives in three runs to lead Atlanta to another win.

The teams return to Minnesota for the final two games. The Braves lead 3–2. Can Atlanta finish the job? Or will the Twins rally now that they are home again?

In the sixth game, Minnesota's best player, Kirby Puckett, takes charge. So far Kirby has had only three hits in the series. But now his team really needs him. His bat comes to life. Then comes his best moment of all . . . .

Atlanta has tied the game to send it into extra innings. Now Kirby leads off the bottom of the eleventh. He swings. B-a-a-m-m-m! The ball sails over the left field wall!

Puckett's homer ties the World Series. The Twins are still alive. The final game will decide the winner. And everyone expects another nail-biter.

The Twins pick veteran Jack Morris to pitch game seven. Morris has never lost a World Series game. But he is pitching with only three days' rest. Fans wonder. How long can he last?

Young John Smoltz will pitch for Atlanta. Smoltz grew up in Michigan. His favorite team was the Detroit Tigers. His favorite player? Jack Morris! Now he will pitch against his idol in the biggest game of his life.

Smoltz and Morris are both great. They match each other pitch for pitch into the late innings. It looks as if one run <u>will</u> win this game.

John Smoltz   Jack Morris

The Braves get their big chance in the eighth. With Lonnie Smith on first, Terry Pendleton hits a drive into the outfield. The speedy Smith should score with ease. But as Smith nears second base, the Twins' second baseman races to the bag. He acts as if Pendleton has hit a ground ball.

Confused, Smith stops running. Then he sees the ball bounce off the wall. He races to third. But he must stop there. Smith cannot score!

The Braves go on to load the bases. But on a grounder to first, the Twins cut down Smith at home. They finish the double play to end the inning. The score stays 0-0.

Now it's the bottom of the eighth. It's the Twins' big chance. They load the bases with one out. But the Braves turn a double play. There's <u>still</u> no score!

For the first time since 1924, the seventh game goes into extra innings. In the bottom of the tenth, Twins left fielder Dan Gladden doubles. He moves to third base. There is only one out.

The Braves walk two players. The bases are loaded. The Braves' outfielders come in close to cut off the run.

Pinch hitter Gene Larkin bats next.
Can he get the job done for the Twins?
B-a-m! He can! He hits a long fly ball over
the outfielders. It bounces and rolls to
the wall. And Gladden trots home with the
Twins' winning score!

The Series is over. Both teams have played their hearts out. Fans are already describing this as the greatest World Series ever.

The 1991 World Series was certainly one of the closest ever. But is it the greatest of all time? That's a question baseball fans will argue over forever. Or at least until next October, when another great World Series begins!